KT-574-476

Have you got them all?

A Note from Enid Blyton's Daughter

Dear Readers,

Enid Blyton wrote *The Naughtiest Girl In The School* when I
was eight years old and it has always been one of my favourites.
It appeared as a serial in Enid Blyton's little magazine called
Sunny Stories, which came out every Friday. My friends and I
would have to wait a whole week before the next chapter came
out. It was the first school story that Enid Blyton had written
and I longed for the proper book to be published.

Enid Blyton was not only a writer for children, she was also
involved in the editing and writing of books for teachers. She
was a trained Froebel and Montessori teacher and had run her
own school before she married.

She was very interested in the world of education and especially
a mixed boarding school called Summerfields, which was opened
by A. S. Neill in 1923. He believed that the school should be
governed by the children themselves with the teachers only taking
part if asked to by the children.

In the *Naughtiest Girl* series, Whyteleafe School is run in the
same way with a meeting held every week in the school hall.
The head boy and girl presided over the meeting aided by twelve
monitors chosen by the other children. It was a kind of school

Parliament, where the children made their own rules, heard grumbles and complaints, judged one another and punished bad behaviour. All problems were discussed and decided by the children and only in very difficult situations were the head teachers asked for their advice.

Of all the school series this is my favourite. The way the school is run has always made me more interested in the characters, and I think, adds to the excitement of the story. I hope you enjoy reading them.

With love from *Gillian*

Gillian (standing) with her sister Imogen and their mother, Enid Blyton

© photo National Magazine Company

Here's The Naughtiest Girl

Enid Blyton

Hodder
Children's
Books

A division of Hachette Children's Books

First published in Great Britain in 1952 by George Newnes

This edition published in 2007 by Hodder Children's Books

For further information on Enid Blyton,
please contact www.blyton.com

14

A Catalogue record for this book is available
from the British Library

ISBN-13: 978 0 340 91772 5

Typeset in Sabon by Avon DataSet Ltd, Bidford-on-Avon, Warks

Printed and bound in Great Britain by Clays Ltd, St Ives plc

The paper and board used in this paperback by Hodder Children's
Books are natural recyclable products made from wood grown in
sustainable forests. The manufacturing processes conform to the
environmental regulations of the country of origin.

Hodder Children's Books
a division of Hachette Children's Books
338 Euston Road, London NW1 3BH
An Hachette UK company
www.hachette.co.uk

Contents

1 Back at Whyteleafe School

It was the summer term at Whyteleafe School. All the children were back again – Elizabeth, Julian, Harry, John, Martin, Rosemary and the rest. They rushed round the school excitedly, glad to be back.

'Summer term! My favourite term!' said Elizabeth Allen, pleased. 'Hi, Julian – come and look at my new tennis racket!'

Julian came over, humming a little song. His green eyes twinkled at Elizabeth. 'Hallo,' he said. 'What are you going to be this term, Elizabeth? Naughtiest girl in the school? Best girl? Silliest?'

Elizabeth laughed and gave Julian a punch. 'I'm a monitor, as you jolly well know,' she said. 'I'm going to do my best, and be a monitor all the term – not be chucked out in the middle, as I was last term. What about *you*?'

'Oh, I'm going to do my best, too – but I've got all sorts of bests,' said Julian, grinning. 'I'll beat you at work this term, for one thing – and I'll beat you at tennis – and I'll beat you at thinking out a few little tricks to make life cheerful – and . . . '

'Oh, Julian – I *hope* you'll think of a few tricks,' said Elizabeth. 'But please don't put sneezing powder in the pages of my books again – honestly, it's awful to *have* to keep on and on sneezing without stopping.'

'Right,' said Julian, 'I'll make a note of it!'

Elizabeth was just going to say something more when she caught sight of a boy in the distance. He was so like Julian that she stared in surprise. Same black untidy hair, same green eyes – but what a sulky face!

'Look – there's somebody who looks very like you,' said Elizabeth. 'He must be a new boy.'

Julian turned. 'Yes – that's a cousin of mine. He's got rather a big opinion of himself, as you'll soon find out. He didn't want to come to Whyteleafe School at all.'

'Why ever not?' said Elizabeth, who simply couldn't *imagine* anyone not wanting to come.

'Well – he's not very fond of *me*,' said Julian. 'He doesn't like people who can do things better than he can – and he'll be in our form.'

'And when you use *your* brains you'll be top whenever you want to!' said Elizabeth. 'Even top of me!'

'That's easy,' said Julian, and got another punch. 'But, quite seriously, Elizabeth, go slow with Patrick – he can be very spiteful. Don't play the heavy monitor with him too soon or too much.'

'I shall tick him off if he doesn't toe the line,' said Elizabeth at once. 'How will he behave, do you think?'

'A bit like *you* behaved when you first came!' said Julian, twinkling at her. 'Don't you remember? You were the Naughtiest Girl in the School – and you meant to be, too! The things you did!'

Elizabeth went bright pink. 'You needn't keep reminding me of that first term,' she said. 'I was awful. I just can't think how I could have behaved like that.'

'Well, I wasn't there then,' said Julian, 'but I've heard plenty about it. I bet you'll always be known as the Naughtiest Girl, even if you go on being a monitor for the rest of your school days and end up as head girl!'

'Gosh – I'd never be that,' said Elizabeth. 'Whoever heard of a Naughtiest Girl ending up as head? Here comes your cousin, Julian.'

Julian swung round. 'Hallo, Patrick,' he said. 'Finding your way about a bit? This is Elizabeth. She's a friend of mine and if you want any help in anything, go to her, because she's a monitor.'

'I'm not likely to go to any friend of yours for help!' said Patrick in a high-and-mighty voice. 'And, by the way, you don't need to spread around the news that I'm your cousin – I'm not really proud of having you for a cousin! Too swollen-headed for my taste!'

He went off, hands in pockets. Julian glared after him. 'If he wasn't new I'd shake him till his teeth rattled!' he said.

Elizabeth was indignant, too. 'What a cheek from a new boy!' she said. 'Well, he won't cheek *me*! If he does I'll report him.'

A bell rang just then, and everyone hurried in to a meal. Elizabeth scrambled for her place at the table. She beamed round at everyone. How good it was to be back among all her friends! John Terry grinned at her across the table.

'Going to help in the garden this term?' he called. 'Have you seen all the seeds that have come up since last term? We shall have a fine show this summer.'

John was partly responsible for the gardens of the school. He loved gardening and was very good at it. Elizabeth nodded back at him. 'Yes – of course I'll help. I love messing about in the garden.'

Elizabeth was going to be busy this term! She meant to ride each day on one of the school ponies. She meant to practise her tennis hard and get into one of the school teams. She meant to help John with the gardens. She was determined to beat Julian as top of the form whenever she could, and that meant a lot of hard work – and she meant to be a good monitor.

Somebody else meant to beat Julian, too! That was Patrick, his cousin. Patrick was jealous of Julian – he had always been glad when he had heard that his cousin didn't work hard at school, and had continually been bottom. He knew that

Julian had good brains, and it pleased him that he hadn't used them.

All the same, he hadn't wanted to go to Whyteleafe School. 'Mixed boys and girls!' he thought, scornfully. 'I'd rather go to an all-boys' school. Look at that Elizabeth now – fancy me having to take orders from a girl! Well – I shan't pay much attention to *her,* anyway!'

He set himself to make a good impression on the others in his form. He entered into everything, and because he was good at games, and could be very comical when he tried, he was soon well-liked.

He hadn't Julian's gift of making extra-ordinary noises – but how he wished he had! Julian could cluck exactly like a hen laying an egg – he could buzz like a bluebottle fly, drone like a bumble-bee, and make very strange noises like nothing at all.

Patrick had often tried to imitate noises, but he couldn't. For one thing everyone knew he was making them, and that gave the game away.

'Nobody ever knows that Julian is doing the noises,' thought Patrick enviously. 'Last Christmas, when he came to us for a party, he imitated a dog whining, and we all hunted round the house for ages – and though I looked and looked at Julian, I *couldn't* see a single movement of his mouth or throat.'

Patrick soon found that Whyteleafe wasn't at all the 'sissy' kind of school he had expected. His class worked hard and played hard, practically every boy or girl had a hobby, and if anything went wrong it was reported at the big Meeting held by the school each week.

This was a kind of Parliament, at which everything was discussed frankly by the children themselves. Complaints were heard, grumbles were made and set right, money was distributed evenly, plans were made.

Rita and William, the head boy and head girl, presided. If punishments had to be meted out, they said what they were to be. Twelve monitors sat on the platform with them – a kind of jury, Elizabeth always thought. She was very proud to be on the platform, sitting alongside the twelve other monitors.

At first Patrick had been pleased to hear that he was to be in Julian's form. He had frequently heard his father and mother say what a pity it was that a boy with good brains like Julian should so often be bottom. He didn't know that the term before Julian had begun to use his brains well, and could always be top of the form if he wanted to be!

So it was a shock to him to find that in the first week's marks Julian was top, Elizabeth was second, and he was tied third with somebody else.

'I thought you made a point of being at the bottom of the form,' he said to Julian. 'Or so I always heard.'

'You heard right,' said Julian, quite amiably. 'I just didn't happen to want to be top, that was all. But I do now. Did *you* want to be top, Patrick? Bad luck that I happen to be using my brains this term, isn't it?'

Patrick turned away. All right – he'd work harder still. He wasn't going to play second fiddle to Julian. He pondered over his tennis. He was good at that. He would take special coaching and practise hard – Julian wasn't much good at tennis! It would do him good to be taken down a peg!

Then one day he came up against Elizabeth.

She was the only person in the form he didn't try to be nice to. She was Julian's friend and a monitor – that was enough for Patrick! He hardly ever addressed a word to her, and if ever she came up to a group he was with he walked away.

Elizabeth laughed at first, but soon it infuriated her. She longed to pull him up for something, but the chance didn't come for three weeks.

Then a notice was put on the board for a meeting. 'Meeting of the Garden Committee, at five o'clock sharp,' said the notice. 'All the first form must attend as well, as volunteers are wanted to help with the weeding.'

Patrick was in the first form. He saw the notice and ignored it. Why should he go? He wasn't interested in gardening, he hated weeding, and he certainly wasn't going to volunteer to do anything in the gardens!

He went off to have a quiet practise by himself, taking his racket and tennis balls with him. There was a wall at the side of the school against which he could hit the balls and strike them continually on the rebound.

So, when the meeting gathered, Patrick was not there! John, who was in charge, looked round. 'Are we all here?' he said.

'No. Patrick isn't,' said Elizabeth at once. 'I bet I know where he is, too! Practising hitting balls against the side-wall. I saw him pass the window with his racket.'

'Oh! Well, he's got to come,' said John. 'You are a monitor, Elizabeth. Fetch him, will you?'

'Right,' said Elizabeth, pleased at being able to make Patrick 'toe the line' for once. 'I can hear the thud-thud of the balls against the wall now. I'll bring him along at once!'

And off she went, quite sure she could make Patrick obey her!

2 Patrick comes up against Elizabeth

Elizabeth hurried round to the side of the school. Thud, thud, thud, she heard the balls being hit regularly against the wall.

She turned the corner and called out to Patrick. 'Hey! You're supposed to be at the Garden meeting. You'd better come at once.'

'Get out of my way, please,' said Patrick. 'I'm practising.'

Elizabeth glared. 'John sent me,' she said.

'All right. I send you back,' said Patrick, almost hitting Elizabeth with one of the balls, as he sent it against the wall near her.

'Don't be an idiot,' said Elizabeth, trying not to lose her temper. 'You know I'm a monitor, don't you? Well, you've *got* to come when you're told. It's no good having monitors unless they're obeyed, you know that.'

'I'm not obeying a girl,' said Patrick. 'Do go away. I shall get annoyed with you in a minute.'

Elizabeth promptly proceeded to get even more annoyed with the infuriating Patrick. She rushed at him and wrenched away his racket. He was so taken by surprise that he let it slip out of his hands.

Then Elizabeth raced away at top speed with it! Patrick tore after her in a rage. Elizabeth turned a corner and deftly threw the racket into the middle of a bush. Then on she went without stopping, back to the meeting.

She arrived there, panting. Before she could say a word to the startled meeting, Patrick arrived, too, fuming. 'Where's my racket? How *dare* you snatch it like that? Elizabeth, what have you done with my racket?'

Elizabeth said nothing. John looked surprised, but pointed to a seat. 'Sit down, Patrick,' he said. 'We've been waiting for you.'

'I haven't come to your silly meeting,' said Patrick, furiously. 'I've come after Elizabeth for my racket!'

'*Sit down*,' ordered John. 'You're at the meeting now, and here you'll stay. You won't get your racket till the meeting is over – and not then if you don't behave yourself!'

Patrick was so surprised at John's determined voice that he sat down. He looked all round for his racket, making up his mind to snatch it and go. But he couldn't see it, which was not surprising, as it was still outside in the bushes!

Patrick didn't hear a word of the meeting. He glared at Elizabeth's triumphant face. He scowled at the little smile on Julian's. Julian was amused at Elizabeth's method of bringing his unwilling cousin to the meeting, and he wondered where she had put the racket.

Elizabeth forgot about Patrick in her interest in the meeting. She was very fond of gardening, and John regarded her as one of his right-hand helpers. He kept consulting her, and she was pleased.

She didn't notice that the sky had clouded over and that it had begun to rain. It was only when it suddenly pelted against the window that she looked out and saw the torrents of rain that were falling. Even then she didn't think about the racket outside in the bushes.

She didn't think of it till the meeting was over. Then John turned to the bored and sulky Patrick. 'Now you can have your racket back from Elizabeth,' he said. 'And please remember if a meeting of the whole form is arranged, you've got to come to it.'

Patrick scowled. Elizabeth suddenly remembered where she had put his racket – in the middle of the bushes. Goodness – had it got wet in the rain? She knew it was a new racket, and that Patrick was intensely proud of it.

She wished she could go and get it out of the bushes and dry it before she gave it to Patrick. But he gave her no chance to do that. He followed close at her heels when she went out of the room. She walked out of the garden door and went to the wet bushes. It was still pouring with rain. She fished out the soaked racket.

Patrick stared at it in horror and anger. 'You beast! You flung my new racket there in the pouring rain! It'll be ruined.'

'It wasn't raining when I put it there, you know it wasn't,' said Elizabeth.

'Well, why didn't you go out and get it when the rain began?' said Patrick furiously. 'You left it there on purpose! You *meant* the rain to spoil it! Just like a girl!'

'I *didn't* mean to spoil it!' said Elizabeth angrily. 'I didn't even notice it was raining till nearly the end of the meeting – and then I forgot all about your racket. It's your fault for not coming to the meeting, so that I had to fetch you!'

Patrick was wiping the strings with his handkerchief. He was trembling with rage and disappointment. His lovely new racket!

'I hate you for this,' he said. 'Now you'll go and laugh about it with Julian, and be glad you've ruined my racket – there wasn't a better one in the school! You'll both be glad it's spoilt!'

'Patrick, don't be silly,' said Elizabeth. 'Look – I'm very sorry I didn't think of your racket being out in the rain. If I'd remembered it, I'd have gone to get it at once. And of *course* Julian and I won't be glad if it's spoilt.'

'Yes, you will. I detest you both,' said Patrick, his face bright red, and his green eyes flaming like Julian's did when he was angry. 'I'll get even with you! You're just exactly the kind of mean, catty girl I'd expect my cocky cousin to be friends with!'

He tucked his racket under his arm, and walked off in a rage, the rain still pouring down as he went. Elizabeth shook back her wet curls. Blow! What an idiot she had been to forget the racket when it began to rain. She really was sorry about that.

Julian met her as she went back. 'Gosh, you *are* wet!' he said. 'What happened? Where did you put his racket? *Not* out in the rain, I hope!'

'Yes, I did – but I didn't mean to,' said Elizabeth, soberly, and she told Julian what had happened, and what Patrick had said. 'He never liked me before, Julian, and now he's really furious with me. He hates you, too, doesn't he? Oh, dear, I do hope he won't do anything silly now. He really looked as if he'd like to hit me with his racket!'

'He probably would have if he hadn't thought his racket would be hurt more than you would!' said Julian. 'Cheer up – what can he do to pay you back – or me either? Nothing that matters. Come on into the gym – there'll be games going on there.'

Patrick made a great fuss about his precious racket. He told everyone what had happened. He spoke of having to get all the strings replaced, and when the next school Meeting was held, he actually got up and asked for the money to have his racket completely restrung!

He stood up when William said, 'Any complaints, please?' Anyone could then stand up and lodge a complaint, big or small. Patrick leapt to his feet before anyone else.

'I have a complaint!' he said. 'Against a monitor, Elizabeth Allen. She left my racket out in the rain and it's ruined. I want to ask for money out of the school money-box so that I can pay for it to be restrung.'

'Elizabeth – perhaps you'd like to say something about this,' said William, the head boy, in surprise.

Elizabeth stood up, feeling embarrassed. She related truthfully what had happened, and added that she was very sorry about the racket being left out in the wet. 'But it wasn't for very long,' she said, 'and I'm sure, William, that it doesn't need restringing.'

'Have you the racket with you?' William

asked Patrick. 'No? Well, go and get it. I know a good bit about rackets and I can tell you at once what wants doing.'

Patrick went to get the racket with a very bad grace. He came back and gave it to William. 'Look – there's a string gone already!' he said, pointing to the broken string. Elizabeth stared in dismay.

William examined the racket very carefully. Then he put it down and looked sternly at Patrick. 'That string is not frayed or split,' he said. 'It has been cut. The racket does not need restringing – only that one string needs putting in. Who cut it, Patrick? Tell me that?'

'How should I know?' said Patrick, sulkily.

There was a short silence. 'Now listen,' said William, 'you yourself must pay for that one string being renewed. The rain had nothing to do with its being broken. I think you know that very well. Every other string is perfectly all right. If you still want the whole racket restrung, you can save up the two pounds you are allowed each week, and pay for it yourself – but it will take you more than a term's money!'

Patrick snatched up his racket without a

word. He glanced at Elizabeth. She looked scornfully back. So he had actually cut a string in his own racket to try and make out that she had really spoilt it by leaving it for a few minutes in the rain! What a thing to do!

Patrick made a sudden face at her, and then left the platform with his racket. He passed by Julian and saw a little smile on his face. He almost hit him with the racket! 'I'll pay you both back!' he said in a whisper, and marched right out of the hall.

'Don't call him back,' said Rita, the head girl, to William. 'He's a new boy. He's got to learn our ways! Now – any more complaints?'

There were none. Nor were there any grumbles. William hammered his fist on the table as a little talking broke out.

'You may dismiss,' he said. 'The Meeting is over.'

Elizabeth sped to Julian. 'Oh, Julian – isn't Patrick MEAN! Did he really cut that string, do you think? It did look exactly as if it had been cut.'

'Of course he did,' said Julian. 'He's an idiot. We'd better look out for him now, Elizabeth.

He may really try to pay you back!'

'Pooh! *I'm* not afraid of Patrick,' said Elizabeth. And she wasn't!

3 Julian's little trick

Patrick brooded over the whole affair. He had a sulky nature; and could not easily forget anything that upset him. He completely ignored Julian and Elizabeth, turning his back on them whenever they came near.

This only amused them, however, and in the end Julian turned the joke against Patrick by calling out warningly whenever he or Elizabeth went near him:

'Be ready to turn your back, Patrick. Here we come again! Hurry up and turn, or you'll see us!'

Patrick tried in vain to think of some big, triumphant way of getting back at Julian and Elizabeth. He was bitterly disappointed that Julian was so good at his class work. His cousin had always been so don't-carish over that, so he had heard, and Patrick had looked forward to crowing over him and being top each week.

But no matter how hard Patrick worked, Julian seemed to be able to work harder! Julian had brilliant brains, found learning easy, and was determined that Patrick should not once beat him in marks.

Patrick was second one week – beating Elizabeth. But Julian was still triumphantly top, a full ten marks ahead of Patrick. Miss Ranger, the class mistress, was amazed at the high marks that Julian, Patrick and Elizabeth showed each week! She didn't know how hard they were vying with one another.

Patrick decided to concentrate on tennis, and beat Julian at that. Julian was good, but he wasn't keen on being in any of the school tennis teams. He said it meant too much hard work to keep in practice!

'All the same, Julian, you'd *better* get some practice in,' said Elizabeth, 'because that cousin of yours is getting jolly good. I watched him playing with some boys older than he is, and he was as good as they were. He'll be in one of the top teams if you don't look out – and won't he crow over you! Do, do beat him, Julian.'

'Blow you, Elizabeth,' said Julian, and pretended to sigh heavily. 'What with working like a slave to keep ahead of you and Patrick in class – and now having to tire myself out with tennis, to beat Patrick, my life's not worth living! What about *you* taking him on at tennis?'

'I do try – but he's got a much harder serve than I have,' said Elizabeth, honestly. 'Go on, Julian – you can be *much* better than Patrick, and I'd jump for joy if you got into the second team, which is what *he* wants to do!'

Julian tried – and Patrick had the disappointment of being well and truly beaten by his cousin when they played against each other two weeks after that! Patrick hadn't realized that Julian had become so good, and he was humiliated and disappointed.

'If Julian gets into the second team instead of me I'll hit him on the head!' thought Patrick, going off the court with a very gloomy face. 'He doesn't really care about tennis, and I do. He's only doing it to spite me.'

'Jolly good, Julian!' said Elizabeth, giving him a thump on the back as he came whistling off the court, having collected all the balls that

Patrick had been too annoyed to pick up. 'Did you see his face? He looked as sick as a hen left out in the rain!'

'Oh well – it's rather a shame really,' said Julian. 'I don't care if I'm good at tennis or not, and he does. But seeing that he only wants to have the pleasure of crowing over me if he beats me, I don't mind beating *him*!'

'Yes – and you *don't* crow!' said Elizabeth. 'I hope you get into the second team and go and play against Hickling Green School, Julian – that's always such a good outing.'

Julian began to get a bit bored with his extra efforts at lessons and tennis. He was also working very hard at making a model aeroplane, for he was very clever with his hands. All this concentration made him feel suddenly stale.

He began to plan a little pleasure for his form. Noises off? Something weird up the chimney? He thought hard, and a sudden grin came on his face.

'The chimney! I sit fairly near the fireplace, and I could work something in the chimney. Now – let's see.'

When his classroom was empty, Julian went

in cautiously. He crouched down by the chimney and looked up it. It was rather narrow. A broad mantelpiece was over the fireplace, and this Julian examined very carefully. He had noticed last winter that, when the wind was in a certain direction, little eddies of smoke came out from under the mantelpiece. He was looking for the crack from which they must have come.

'There must be a crack or a hole somewhere,' thought Julian, 'or the smoke wouldn't get out from the chimney under the mantelpiece and into the room. Ah – here it is!'

He had found the crack, where the cement had worn away. He took a chisel and made the hole considerably bigger. He poked the chisel some way through, and then decided that the hole was big enough for his purpose.

He took a piece of string and tied a penknife to one end. He poked the knife through the hole, and gave it a push. It clattered into the chimney, fell down and suddenly appeared in the hearth!

'Ha! Good!' said Julian, pleased. He still had hold of the string that went into the hole. He knocked a small tack in on the underside of the wooden mantelpiece and then tied the string to it firmly. He tested it. Yes, it held well.

He undid the knife from the other end of the string, which hung down the chimney into the fireplace. He then disappeared into the corridor and fetched a small bell that was kept there to summon Matron if she was needed in a hurry.

He went back into the classroom and carefully tied the bell to the end of the string that hung down the chimney. Then he undid the other end from the nail, and pulled it, so that the bell was dragged out of sight up the chimney!

Then Julian gave a little tug to the string he held, and a muffled and rather weird tinkle came from up the chimney!

Julian chuckled. He ran the end of the string under the mantelpiece and held it in place by little staples he drove into the wood. The string fell down the side of the fireplace just by his chair. Julian sat down and bent over his desk, holding the end of the string in his hand. He tugged it – and a mournful little jingle came from the inside of the chimney!

'A nice little treat for the class this afternoon,'

thought Julian, and tied the string to one leg of his chair.

Miss Ranger took the class that afternoon. It was a geography lesson, rather dull. Julian waited for a moment of silence and then gave the string tied to his chair leg a little tug.

At once it pulled the bell hanging in the chimney and a sudden little jingle sounded in the room. Everyone looked up. Julian did too. He meant to be as surprised as anyone else!

He tugged the string again. Jingle-tinkle-tink went the bell, obligingly.

'What's that noise?' asked Miss Ranger, puzzled. 'It sounds exactly like a bell some-where. Where is it ringing? Has anyone got a bell with them this afternoon?'

'No, Miss Ranger!' chorused everyone except Julian. He tugged again, and the bell jangled quite loudly.

'Well – it *sounds* up the chimney!' said John. 'But how could a bell ring in the chimney?'

'It couldn't,' said Miss Ranger, firmly. 'So we won't ask you or anyone else to go crawling up the chimney to look for bells there, John. Stand up, everyone, and put your hands above your heads. If anyone has a bell, and can ring it when his hands are above his head, he will be clever!'

Everyone stood with hands above their heads, Julian too. Jingle-jingle-jing! The bell rang again. Julian had managed to get his foot to the string and jerk it! A babble of noise broke out at once.

'Nobody's got a bell and yet it rang again! Miss Ranger, what is it? Miss Ranger, it's peculiar! Where is it, do you suppose? Can't we look for it?'

'No,' said Miss Ranger, firmly, imagining a bevy of excited children crawling over the room and completely ruining the rest of the geography lesson. 'Bell or no bell, we go on with the lesson. Sit!'

They sat and the bell immediately rang a merry peal. 'Take no notice,' commanded Miss Ranger, who was just as puzzled as anyone else, but determined not to show it. 'I have only one more thing to say about this bell – and that is, if I find out that anyone in this class is plaguing us with a jingling bell, I shall do a bit of plaguing myself – and the culprit will be very, very sorry for himself!'

After that they all settled down, and although the bell rang plaintively at intervals, and the children began to giggle each time, nobody dared to take much notice of it.

As soon as the class was ended and Miss Ranger was safely out of the room, John ran to the chimney. 'It sounded as if it came from here,' he said. 'I know it did!'

He put his hand up the chimney and groped about. Tinkle, jing! He had touched the bell!

'It *is* up here!' he cried. 'I thought so. But how on earth did it get there?' He turned and saw Julian's grinning face. He laughed. 'Julian! It's one of your ridiculous tricks – but HOW did you get the bell hanging there?'

'Easy!' said Julian, and showed the interested class how he had managed it. Only one of them sneered. That was Patrick, of course.

'What a childish trick! I'm sure Miss Ranger will be very scornful about it when I tell her.'

He was immediately pushed down hard on a chair and three or four children pinned him down firmly.'Sneak! Tell-tale! We'll never speak to you again if you do that.'

'All right, all right. I was only joking,' said

Patrick, trying to push them off, afraid of making them dislike him. They let him go.

John had pulled the bell down from the chimney and now it lay on the floor nearby. Patrick gave it a vicious kick, and it slid jangling over the floor. Julian smiled broadly. 'Taking it out on the bell instead of on me, I suppose?' he said. 'Pity you can't see a joke, Patrick.'

The next day a really peculiar thing happened. It was Miss Ranger's class again, this time in maths. All the children were copying sums down from the blackboard, when once more there was a curious noise from the chimney.

Everyone raised their heads and grinned. Was this another trick of old Julian's? But he looked as surprised as they did.

The noise came again, a struggling kind of noise, then came a series of high squeaks, and a little soot fell down the chimney.

'Now whatever is *this*?' said Miss Ranger, exasperated. She suddenly thought of Julian and his tricks. She looked straight at him. 'Julian – is this one of your tricks? Answer me truthfully, please.'

'No, Miss Ranger. It isn't one of my tricks. I

can't *imagine* what is going on in the chimney,'
said Julian, quite truthfully.

Squeak, squeak, chirri-chirri-chirrup!

Patrick got up. 'Julian's not telling the truth!'
he said. 'It was *his* chimney trick yesterday –
and it's his trick again today! Look up the
chimney and you'll see his trick, Miss Ranger!
He's a frightful fibber!'

4 Patrick in trouble

The whole class stared at Patrick in amazement and disgust. Julian shrugged his shoulders. 'I do assure you, Miss Ranger, I haven't the faintest idea what is going on up our chimney,' he said.

'You DO know! You've put something up there again!' cried Patrick, in a fury. 'Just to suck up to the class and make them think you're marvellous!'

'That's enough,' said Miss Ranger. And then, quite suddenly, with another series of squeaks and chirps, something fell down the chimney and came to rest with a little thud on the hearth!

'Chirrup!' it said, feebly. The children stared at it. 'A baby starling – and golly, here comes another!' cried Harry, as a second black little creature arrived beside the other. 'There must have been a starling's nest up the chimney – and these two have wriggled out and fallen down. Poor little things!'

'Sucks to you, Patrick,' said Elizabeth, in delight. 'You can't say that Julian built the starling's nest or turned out the young starlings, can you! Sucks to you!'

'Elizabeth, I don't like that vulgar expression,' said Miss Ranger, coldly. 'John, take those two poor little creatures and put them outside in a bush where perhaps their starling parents may see them and feed them. Patrick, take that scowl off your face.'

'It was Julian who put the bell up the chimney yesterday, anyhow!' blurted out Patrick. 'So what are you going to do about *that*?'

'Nothing,' said Miss Ranger, calmly. 'Sit down in your places, everyone. We are now going on with our lesson – and I must warn you all that I do NOT feel in the mood for any more disturbances, whispers or giggles.'

The children bent over their books, but there were many scornful glances thrown at Patrick. He bent over his book too, kicking himself for thinking that was a trick of Julian's – and for being unable to prevent himself from blurting out about the bell-trick.

He hurried out in front of the others afterwards, afraid that they would take him to task. He ran to get his racket, meaning to go and bang the balls at the side-wall, to work off some of his anger.

But the class followed him, and soon he was surrounded by an angry little company. Elizabeth advanced on him, her eyes gleaming. 'I may as well tell you,' she began, 'that sooner or later complaints will be made about you at the next school Meeting, and—'

'Shut up,' said Patrick, and threw a ball up into the air to hit against the wall. 'Go away, all of you. I'm fed up with this school – and most of all I'm fed up with my grinning, very-very-clever cousin – and with Elizabeth, the cocky, high-and-mighty monitor!'

Elizabeth tried to grab his racket, to make him stop playing about – he should be *made* to listen to what was being said! But Patrick swung it away and then raised it again to hit another ball.

He hit Elizabeth instead! Crack! The racket

descended heavily on her right shoulder and she yelled. Julian leapt at Patrick, his face blazing. Coward! To hit a girl!

He caught Patrick by the shoulder, and held him tightly. 'We'll call a Meeting tonight!' he said. 'We'll say that for the rest of this term Patrick shall not play tennis again! We'll confiscate his racket for hitting Elizabeth.'

'Let me go!' said Patrick, fiercely. 'It was an accident – but I'm glad I hit her, all the same. She deserved it! Call your Meeting if you like – I shan't be there! And I'll tell you this, Julian – you're only doing this to keep me out of the second team, because you want to be in it yourself, instead of me!'

He flung Julian off, made a dive under the arms held up to stop him, and tore away at top speed.

'Let him go,' said Rosemary. 'Elizabeth, are you hurt?'

'No. Not really,' said Elizabeth. 'Only bruised. Isn't he a beast, though? Julian, it's bad luck on you to have a cousin like that!'

'We'll send him to Coventry! We won't speak to him for the rest of the term! We'll see that he doesn't touch a racket again!' said several voices.

'Telling a fib about Julian!'

'Wasn't it strange, though, those birds falling down the chimney the very day after Julian had put a bell up there!'

'Jolly decent of Miss Ranger not to say anything more about it when Patrick blurted out the truth,' said John.

A monitor from the second form appeared round the corner. 'I say! What's happening? Didn't you hear the bell, you idiots? You won't get anything to eat if you don't hurry up. I've been sent to find you.'

'Oh goodness – we never even *heard* the bell!' said Elizabeth, still rubbing her shoulder. 'Come on, everyone. All this has made me feel jolly hungry.'

Patrick did not come in to the meal. Miss Ranger did not inquire about him. She knew that he was upset and probably did not want to appear in public just then. Nobody bothered about him. Let him miss his meal if he wanted to. Do him good! That was what most of his class thought.

Elizabeth and Julian did not attempt to call a

big school Meeting that night after all. When they had cooled down a bit it seemed rather silly to air the grievances of the first form in front of the whole school.

'After all, the next Meeting is on Saturday,' said Elizabeth. 'If Patrick doesn't behave himself for the rest of the week, we'll make a formal complaint about him then, and deal with him. I don't really believe he *meant* to hit me, Julian.'

'Well, perhaps not,' said Julian. 'He's an unpleasant bit of work, though, isn't he? I wish he hadn't come here. It's hard enough to beat *you* in order to be top of the form – it's getting to be even harder to beat Patrick – and I'm really a bit tired of practising my tennis at every moment, just so that he won't be in the second team!'

'It's jolly good for you to work hard at things!' said Elizabeth, remembering how don't-carish Julian had been the term before. 'I wonder where Patrick is? He hasn't shown up at all.'

'Good thing too,' said Julian. 'I expect he doesn't want to face the form. They'll do to him what he's been doing to you and me – they'll turn their backs whenever he appears!'

'Where did you put his racket?' asked Elizabeth. 'Have you hidden it so that he can't get it?'

'Yes. I've put a note in his desk to say that he can have it back if he apologizes to you,' said Julian. 'Otherwise, he won't have it.'

'Oh, dear – I don't really like all this upset,' said Elizabeth. 'It makes me have feelings that aren't at all suitable to a monitor. Even if Patrick comes and apologizes – and I believe he'd rather lose his racket than do that – I shan't feel like accepting his apology. I might say something rude and begin the upset all over again.'

'Well, do,' said Julian with a grin. 'I've no objection!'

'Come and have a game of tennis,' said Elizabeth. 'Let's slash out at the balls and work some of our crossness out of us. Come on!'

So out they went and were soon hitting the balls with a will. When they had finished they looked about for Patrick. Would he come and apologize? He must have seen the note in his desk by now.

But he was still nowhere to be seen!

5 At midnight

The children were allowed to take their tea into the garden that day and have little picnics in friendly groups. That was always fun. Elizabeth, Julian, John, Harry, Rosemary and Joan found a place in the shade by some bushes.

'Anyone seen Patrick?' asked Elizabeth, biting into bread and honey.

'Yes. I saw him coming out of our classroom,' said John. 'I don't know where he is now though. Having tea by himself somewhere, I expect, brooding over his woes.'

'Oh, well – don't let's think about him any more,' said Elizabeth. 'He's keeping out of our way and I'm not surprised.'

They thought no more about Patrick. Elizabeth went back with the others to fetch her prep and do it out-of-doors that lovely warm evening. But it was difficult to learn French verbs when the swallows swooped and darted in the sky, and bees hummed happily in the flowers around. French verbs didn't go well with swallows and bees.

When they all went up to bed Elizabeth looked round once more for Patrick. She hated to go to bed without making up a quarrel, though she had often done so.

She called to Julian as he went to the boys' dormitory. 'Julian! See if Patrick is in your dormy.'

He wasn't. Julian began to feel a bit worried. Where was the idiot? Sulking somewhere? He debated whether or not to report that Patrick hadn't come up to bed. He decided that he wouldn't – not for a little while, anyhow.

'If I do report him, and he's hiding some-where, waiting till we're all in bed because he's afraid of being jeered at, he'll get into more trouble,' thought Julian. 'And he'll think I've reported him just for that reason – to get him into a row. Blow him! Well, I'll get into bed, and wait till he comes before I go to sleep.'

He told this to John and Harry, who shared the dormy with him and Patrick. They agreed to do the same as Julian – wait till Patrick came before they went to sleep. 'And we won't rag him at all,' said Harry. 'He's had a pretty poor day.'

But – alas for their good resolves – every boy was fast asleep before five minutes had gone! The girls fell asleep, too – but Elizabeth kept waking up and wondering about Patrick.

As she turned over for about the twelfth time, she thought she heard a rustling of paper. She sat up in bed and groped for what she had heard. Yes – there *was* a bit of paper somewhere in her bed. It must have slipped down there when she had got in. She pulled it out.

She put on her light and read what was written there. It was a note from Patrick!

ELIZABETH,

You can believe me or not, but I didn't *mean* to hit you, and I apologize for my racket slipping down on your shoulder like that. It was partly your fault for grabbing at it. I wish I hadn't blurted out about Julian's trick, too, but I said it without thinking.

You won't be bothered with me any more. I'm fed up with Whyteleafe and I'm going away tonight as soon as it's dark. I'm going home. It was mean to take my racket away from me. I would have liked to take it with me. There's no use in staying at Whyteleafe – Julian is determined to out-do me in everything – but the tennis isn't fair, because I really *could* do well at that, and I might have got into the second team.

Nobody likes me now. I don't like any-body either, least of all you. I hope there's a good old upset about me running away – it will serve this beastly school right!

PATRICK

Elizabeth read this in the greatest horror. She sat staring at the letter in a panic. Patrick must have slid it under the sheet for her to find it when she got into bed, and it had slipped down when she got in. What a pity she hadn't read it hours before – she might have stopped Patrick from being such an idiot as to run away!

She slipped on her dressing-gown and went to Julian's dormy. She put her head round the door and called softly: 'Julian! Julian!'

Julian was a light sleeper. He awoke at once. He went to the door. 'What are you doing here?' he said. 'You'll get into a frightful row.'

'It's about Patrick,' said Elizabeth. 'Come down into our classroom and read a note he's left in my bed. It's urgent, Julian.'

Julian put on his dressing-gown and the two went down into their classroom. They did not dare to switch on the light, but shone their torches on to the note. Julian read it in dismay.

'I say! The fathead! We'll have the police looking for him, and Whyteleafe in the papers, and there'll be a frightful disturbance,' he groaned. 'What in the world are we to do?'

'When do you suppose he went?' whispered Elizabeth. 'He wouldn't go till it was dark, would he? It can't have been dark very long because these summer nights are light for ages. Should we snoop round a bit and see if we can see anything of him?'

'We could. But he'll be gone,' said Julian, feeling most uncomfortable at the thought of having to go and wake Mr Johns and the two headmistresses, and show them the note. He began to feel that he hadn't come very well out of the affair himself. It was possible that the grown-ups might think him rather mean to have deliberately tried to out-shine Patrick, and not give him a chance to make good at anything.

There was no sign of Patrick, so the two decided most reluctantly to go and tell someone in authority. They made their way down the back stairs of the school, meaning to go through to the hall and up the stairs to where the staff bedrooms were.

And then, as they went down the back stairs, they heard a sound. They stopped. What was that? Where did it come from?

'It's in the cupboard,' whispered Julian. 'Look – over there, where all the sports things are kept. But Patrick can't be there!'

Another sound came from the cupboard – a sound as if the door was being jiggled a little. The two crept up to it. The key was in the lock. Julian did not touch the key, but cautiously turned the handle. The door would not open. It was obviously locked on the outside.

'Whoever's in there is locked in,' whispered

Julian. They looked at one another. 'It can't be Patrick. He wouldn't go to this cupboard – it's only got spare sports things in.'

Julian spoke quietly at the crack of the door. 'Who's in here?'

A voice answered at once. ' Who's that? I'm locked in here. I'm Patrick. Let me out.'

Elizabeth clutched at Julian joyfully. So Patrick hadn't gone! Julian was glad, too. He put his mouth to the crack again.

'Patrick. It's me, Julian – and Elizabeth's here, too. We found your note just now. You're an idiot. We are idiots, too, so we're quits.'

There was a silence. 'You let me out at once,' came Patrick's voice, rather shaky.

'All right – on one condition,' said Julian. 'Do you promise to give up your mad idea of running off tonight, and will you go straight to bed?'

'No,' said Patrick.

'All right. We're off to bed,' said Julian.

A frantic voice came from inside the cupboard. 'Don't go! It's horrible in here – smelly and lonely and uncomfortable. Let me out. I won't run off. I promise.'

'How did you get locked in here?' asked Julian, still not turning the key.

'Well – I badly wanted to take my racket with me,' said Patrick's voice, 'and I didn't know where it had been hidden. So I looked everywhere. The last place I thought of was this old sports cupboard – but while I was looking someone came along, slammed the door and locked me in.'

'Matron, I expect,' said Julian. 'She's always slamming doors and locking them. Well – I'll let you out.'

He unlocked the door and shone his torch into the cupboard. Patrick was there, blinking, looking very tousled and untidy, and rather white in the face.

Elizabeth felt sorry for him. She slid her arm through his. 'Patrick! I know you didn't mean to hit me! Of *course* I know it. I think we all got silly and excited. We none of us behaved very well.'

'You didn't come to any meals,' said Julian, remembering. 'Aren't you hungry?'

'Yes,' said Patrick going upstairs with them.

'Come and have some of my tuck, then,' said

Julian. 'But don't give me away, because we're not supposed to have food at night. Elizabeth, look the other way. Being a monitor, you can't approve!'

'Oh, dear – can't I? But I *do*,' said Elizabeth. 'Patrick, I'll give you back your racket.'

She disappeared. The boys looked at one another. Julian shoved some more biscuits at Patrick. 'I don't *really* want to be in the second team,' said Julian, in a casual, ordinary voice. 'I just thought I would be to show you I *could* be. But all this practising bores me. In any case, you'll always be better than me in that. So go ahead.'

'Oh! Well, thanks,' said Patrick, seeing that this was Julian's way of patching up a quarrel. 'And *I* don't particularly want to slave to be top of the form. You're welcome to that position. We'll – er – split our brains, shall we?'

'Not a bad idea,' said Julian, munching a biscuit himself. 'Easier for us both. Hullo, here's Elizabeth back again.'

Elizabeth came in with the racket.

'Here you are, Patrick – and don't you dare hit me again with it!'

Patrick eagerly took his precious racket. Elizabeth suddenly realized what a tremendous lot he thought of it. She stared at him and he stared back. Then he suddenly smiled.

'Whatever would people think if they saw us all here, munching biscuits at this time of night!' he said. 'Now, don't you go reporting us at the next Meeting, Elizabeth!'

'Come on – we *must* go to bed!' said Julian hearing the clock strike midnight. 'We shall all be bottom of the form if we go on like this – staying up till past midnight!'

They crept upstairs very quietly and said goodnight on the landing. Elizabeth got into bed feeling at peace. Who would have thought things would turn out like this after all? Perhaps Patrick would settle down and be as proud of Whyteleafe as they all were.

Julian got into bed and was asleep at once. Patrick was in bed, too – but he was rather uncomfortable: he had taken his racket with him, feeling that he really couldn't let it out of his sight now; and it was a very hard and knobbly bed-fellow!

'Whyteleafe School's not so bad,' thought

Patrick. 'Julian's not so bad, either. And as for Elizabeth, why, she's really quite nice. I'm very much afraid – *very* much afraid – I'm going to like her!'

If you can't wait
to read more about
The Naughtiest Girl,
then turn over for
the beginning of her
next adventure...

The Naughtiest Girl Keeps a Secret

1 A message from William and Rita

'It's still lovely and sunny!' said Elizabeth happily, as she came out of the first form classroom with her friend Julian and his cousin, Patrick.

It was four o'clock in the afternoon. Lessons at Whyteleafe School had finished for the day. Along the corridor, boys and girls were bursting out of other classrooms, laughing and chattering noisily. Soon everyone would change out of school uniform, go to tea, then race off to take part in all their summer term activities.

There was always so much to do at Whyteleafe, thought Elizabeth. She loved it here now. She was still a monitor, though only an honorary one this term. There were no silly quarrels to worry about at present, no misunderstandings, no having to keep her temper. She and Patrick were just starting to get on reasonably well too. At the beginning of term they had been sworn enemies.

'This is my favourite time of year!' Elizabeth told Julian. 'The evenings are so light and long. It gives you time to fit everything in. I think I'll do some gardening later. I'm sure my lettuces need watering . . .'

'You've got to come and watch my tennis match first,' Patrick butted in.

Elizabeth nodded that she would, then continued. 'To think how much I hated it here at the beginning. It seems so strange now. I did everything I could to try and get myself sent home.'

'You mean, last summer, when you were the naughtiest girl in the school?' asked Julian, his green eyes showing his amusement. 'Wish I'd been here then. Poor Elizabeth. You've been trying to live it down ever since.'

'Well, I *have* lived it down,' said Elizabeth firmly.

'She wouldn't be a monitor if she hadn't,' Patrick pointed out. 'Anyway, it wasn't all that strange. Hating it here at the beginning, I mean.

Look at me: three weeks ago I couldn't stand the place!'

It was true. Julian's cousin was new this term. And, although the two cousins looked rather alike, their characters were very different. Julian was lively and jokey, full of a self-confidence which came from being so clever and good at everything. He didn't, for example, in the least mind Elizabeth being a monitor. Patrick, when he'd first arrived, had been sullen and lacking in confidence. And he had deeply resented a girl telling him what to do.

'But you do like it here now, don't you, Patrick?' said Elizabeth.

'Not so terrible having a school with girls in it, is it?' said Julian, wryly. 'And you've got your trial for the second tennis team. Already! I call that good going.'

'Yes, not bad.' Patrick flushed with pride. 'Don't you two forget to come and watch me, either. I need supporters.'

'We'll come and support you,' piped up a voice in the corridor, just behind them. It was Arabella Buckley, with a friend. 'We'll come and cheer Patrick on, won't we, Rosemary?'

'Of course we'll come!' said Rosemary, who always agreed with everything Arabella said.

'We'll be there, Patrick,' said Elizabeth quietly. 'You know you can do it. I'm sure you can beat Roger.'

Roger Brown was a big boy, in his last term at Whyteleafe. But even so, he was only clinging on to his place in the school's second team by his fingertips.

Mr Warlow, the sports master, had watched Patrick play. He had also noted how hard the new boy practised each day. So a trial had been arranged.

After tea today, Roger and Patrick were to play singles against each other. Everybody knew that if Patrick proved to be the stronger player, he would be awarded that precious place in the second team.

'You'll need that special racket of yours though, Patrick,' said Julian. 'Better not let Elizabeth get anywhere near it. You know what she's like.'

He kept a straight face as he said it. For a moment Elizabeth took him seriously.

'Julian Holland, what a hateful thing to say—'

Once, in a fit of rage with Patrick, Elizabeth had caused his lovely new racket to get soaked with rain. She hated to be reminded of it now.

It was Patrick who quickly smoothed things over. 'Don't worry! I'll guard it with my life!' he smiled.

Elizabeth smiled then, too, and the awkward moment passed.

At teatime, she even managed to make a joke at her own expense.

Patrick had changed into his tennis things and come over to join Elizabeth's table, carrying his precious tennis racket. It really was his pride and joy.

'If anything can bring me luck, it's this,' he told John McTavish. 'I'm useless with any other racket.'

'Better not leave it by my chair then, Patrick,' said Elizabeth. 'I think you ought to padlock it to the table leg. You know what I'm like!'

All the boys and girls at the table laughed. Julian gave Elizabeth's arm an approving pinch.

He was pleased to see his friend not taking herself too seriously.

Arabella, however, turned her pretty little doll-like face towards Patrick and smiled primly.

'It wasn't so funny at the time, though, was it, Patrick?' she said.

Elizabeth ground her teeth.

She tried hard to think of something clever to say, to get back at Arabella.

But at that moment, someone came hurrying over to their table.

'Elizabeth?'

'Joan!'

Elizabeth was always pleased to see her special friend. But Joan was older and had gone up to the second form quite quickly, so the two girls saw less of each other these days. Elizabeth knew that if she did well at lessons this term she, too, would go up in September. Then she and Joan would be together again. Elizabeth was looking forward to that.

'I've got a message for you,' said Joan softly. She was always quietly spoken. 'It's from William and Rita. They would like you to come along to their study after tea, please.'

Elizabeth frowned in surprise. William and Rita were the head boy and the head girl of Whyteleafe School.

'Are you coming too? Are all the monitors coming?' Elizabeth asked.

She was puzzled because there was no school Meeting due for a day or two yet.

Sometimes all the monitors were called in if there were something important to discuss before the Meeting. The Meeting was held once a week. All pupils had to attend. It was a kind of Parliament. At Whyteleafe it was the boys and girls themselves who made many of the important rules and saw that they were applied fairly. When problems arose, they sorted them out themselves. The teachers rarely had to be involved.

'No, they just want you,' said Joan. 'I don't know what it's about.'

Elizabeth rushed through her tea after that. What did William and Rita want to see her about?

'Hey, Monitor, don't gobble your food. You're supposed to set a good example,' teased Julian. 'William and Rita aren't going to disappear down a big hole. They can wait,' he added, carelessly.

'I'll finish up your scrambled egg if you can't manage it all, Elizabeth,' said her friend Kathleen, all smiles and rosy cheeks as usual.

'Would you really like it?' asked Elizabeth, gratefully. 'Cook's given me too much. Then I can slip off and see what they want with me. I haven't done anything bad lately, have I, Kathleen?'

She picked up her remaining chocolate biscuits, put them in her pocket, scraped her chair back, then got up and left the table.

'If you'd done anything bad it would have to wait for the Meeting, Elizabeth!' Julian called after her, 'and the whole school would have to hear about it. You know that's the system here. See you later!'

'Come straight on to the tennis-courts!' Patrick added. 'I'll be playing soon.'

But Elizabeth, hurrying out of the hall, didn't hear them. The chatter and clatter from other tables filled her ears and drowned out the boys' voices.

There was only one thought in her mind at present.

Why had the head boy and girl asked her to come and see them?

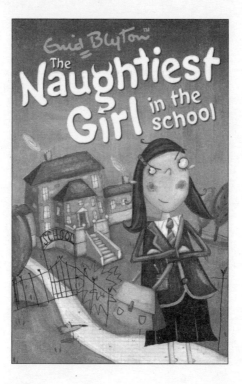

Elizabeth Allen is spoilt, mischievous and determined
to get home – whatever the cost – she really is the
Naughtiest Girl in the school! Exciting stories about
the girls and boys boarding at Whyteleafe School.

For the full range of Naughtiest Girl books and eBooks, please see
www.hodderchildrens.co.uk

Enid Blyton

Celebrate 70 years of

The Famous Five

These special edition jackets of the first five books have been brought to you by Quentin Blake and friends in support of the House of Illustration.

CHRIS RIDDELL

OLIVER JEFFERS

Quentin Blake

Helen Oxenbury

Emma Chichester Clark

www.famousfivebooks.com
www.houseofillustration.org.uk

Enid Blyton

THE
FAMOUS FIVE'S
SURVIVAL GUIDE

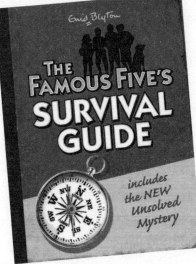

Packed with useful information on surviving outdoors and solving mysteries, here is the one mystery that the Famous Five never managed to solve. See if you can follow the trail to discover the location of the priceless Royal Dragon of Siam.

The perfect book for all fans of mystery, adventure and the Famous Five!

ISBN 9780340970836

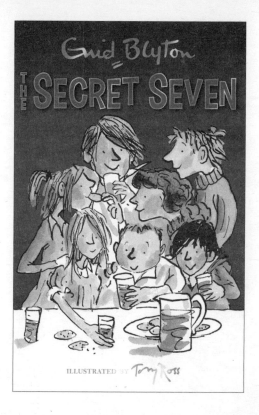

Meet Peter, Janet and Jack, Barbara, Pam, Colin and George. Together they are The Secret Seven — ready to solve any mystery, anytime! A great introduction to adventure stories.

For the full range of Secret Seven books and eBooks, please see
www.hodderchildrens.co.uk